The Dewavery Way

Family Meeting Hour

By Cynthia Dewindt

Illustrated by Darja Kudrjavceva

To order additional copies of this book, contact:
Xlibris
844-714-8691
www.Xlibris.com
Orders@Xlibris.com

ISBN: Softcover   979-8-3694-2023-2
        Hardcover   979-8-3694-2024-9
        EBook   979-8-3694-2022-5

Library of Congress Control Number: 2024908053

Print information available on the last page

Rev. date: 04/25/2024

ClaireBear

JaJa

BJ

Acknowledgements:

To my three children, Cee Cee, Jalil and BJ

One Saturday morning, Ms. Carol told ClaireBear to do the laundry. It was JaJa and BJ's job to assist her that day. When ClaireBear was a small child, she watched her mother clean their clothes.

By the time she was ten years old, ClaireBear knew how to do the laundry very well on her own. It was always important to ClaireBear to do a good job. "Ok, boys, said Ms. Carol, help your sister and pay attention to everything she does so that you will learn."

ClaireBear asked JaJa and BJ to help her put the clothes into the washing machine, but they did not hear her. As usual, they were too busy playing around, instead of listening. This was the last straw for ClaireBear. She finally had enough of JaJa and BJ goofing around while she did all the work.

With her hands on her hips, ClaireBear approached her brothers. She yelled, "Mommy said that y'all have to work too, so stop playing and come on and help me." Embarrassed and annoyed, the boys helped ClaireBear with the laundry until it was all done.

The next evening, it was JaJa's turn to do the dishes after dinner. JaJa knew how to do the dishes well, but this time he rushed to do them to return to his video game. There were several dishes in the dish rack that were not properly cleaned.

ClaireBear noticed the uncleaned dishes and told JaJa to clean them. He refused. "Why don't you clean them for me," he said. "Nope, I did the dishes last night. Now it's your turn. You better clean those dishes before Dad sees it," argued ClaireBear.

"You're so annoying," said JaJa. "And you're lazy," said ClaireBear. "Leave me alone. You're not my boss. I can't stand you," said JaJa. "Oh yeah, well, I'm not going to do the dishes for you this time. From now on, you're on your own," yelled ClaireBear. "Get out of my room," screamed JaJa. ClaireBear left JaJa's room very angry. Her face was flushed.

Knowing his father would soon come in the kitchen to put the dishes away, JaJa rushed back to the sink to clean the dishes properly. He did not want to upset his father, and that was more important to him than playing his video game. He knew that ClaireBear was right, but that didn't stop him from being irritated by her.

ClaireBear, JaJa, and sometimes BJ had been fussing and fighting for weeks. They would find reasons to argue.

Later that evening, Ms. Carol told Mr. Bob that she was concerned about the children not getting along. "I agree with you, Carol. It's normal for brothers and sisters to get on each other's nerves, but their quarreling has been out of control lately," said Mr. Bob.

With a heavy heart, Ms. Carol said, "Bob, I think the problem might be partly our fault. ClaireBear is the oldest, and she had to learn quickly how to be a good helper. She probably feels that JaJa and BJ are not doing their part in household chores or at least not taking it seriously enough."

14

"I understand, said Mr. Bob. After work tomorrow, I will have a talk with JaJa and BJ about responsibility. Afterward, if you have any ideas on bringing back the peace between them, then let me know."
"Ok, Bob, " said Ms. Carol. I will let you know."

As promised, Mr. Bob came home from work the next day and began to speak to his sons. He said, "JaJa, BJ, everyone plays an important part in our family. What one person does affect the whole family. JaJa, you are BJ's older brother. It is your responsibility to lead by a good example. So, JaJa, I understand that there are certain chores around the house that you don't like to do. Is that correct?" Asked Mr. Bob. "Yes, sir. Why should I have to help ClaireBear with the laundry? It doesn't take three people to do laundry, besides, she is better at it," said JaJa.

That's a good question, JaJa. You're right, it doesn't take three people to do laundry. However, there are five of us in this house, and laundry has to be done often, and that's a shared responsibility. The reason that you and BJ are there to assist ClaireBear is so that you can learn and become just as good as she is at doing so.

"There is another reason why we require the three of you to do laundry together," said Mr. Bob. "What's that Dad?" Asked BJ. Mr. Bob responded, "It's because, in life, you have to be able to work as a team. That's whether you own your own business, or someone employs you. Learning to work well with others starts right here at home. You are being trained on how to be a good leader and how to be a good follower in the outside world."

"One more thing, and this is probably your most important lesson. There will be things in life that you don't like to do or want to do. We don't run away from our responsibilities. First, do what you must do so that you can later do what you want to do. Remember, even when no one is looking, your name is attached to everything you do. Respect yourself enough and those around you to do your best regardless of the job. Do you understand?" Mr. Bob asked in a firm voice. "Yes sir," said JaJa and BJ. "Good, now start doing better," said Mr. Bob.

20

After speaking to his sons, Mr. Bob and Ms. Carol labored for hours over how to help their children bring peace back home. Finally, they came up with a plan.

The following Sunday, Mr. Bob and Ms. Carol told the children to come into the family room. Mr. Bob began to speak. "Your mother and I are concerned about your behavior towards each other lately. As a result, we decided to have a family meeting hour every Sunday. We will call it FMH for short. During the week, you will pay attention to everything positive that your siblings are doing or saying. Then, on Sunday, you will be required to face your brother or sister and tell them what you noticed about them that was good.

If you comment with an attitude, you will be required
to give two more true compliments to that person.
You must pay attention all week long to each other
so that you will have something good to say about
each other. If you come to the meeting unprepared
or refuse to give a comment, then you will not
be forced to do so. Instead, you will not get your
allowance that week. That money will be given
or divided to those who did well during FMH."

"May I ask why we have to do this?" ClaireBear asked. Before answering her question, Ms. Carol held up a white paper and put a little black dot in the center of the page. She asked the children, "What do you see?" They all said, "a little black dot." Mr. Bob asked them if they saw anything else. The children all said no. Ms. Carol said, "That's why we are having FMH once a week. It is because it's easy to zero in on what we believe is a problem with someone and not look at the whole person. In this case, you all focused on a tiny black dot and paid no attention to all the white surrounding it. FMH is not a punishment for you guys. Instead, it is an exercise for you to pay more attention to the good in each other."

28

While listening to his parents, JaJa felt gloomy. His head and shoulders began to fall. ClaireBear was not happy with this news either. She rested her face in her hand and hoped that this was a bad dream. Once the meeting was over, JaJa said, "I can't believe I have to say something nice about you. This is going to be too hard." "I agree," said ClaireBear. "I'm just going to go along with it because I don't want you to get part of my allowance." As for BJ, the idea of FMH did not bother him as much. He looked up to his brother and sister, so he could easily say something nice about them.

During the week, the children went about their regular routine. The first few days, they had forgotten about FMH. However, when it started getting close to Sunday, they nervously started paying attention to each other and looking for good things to say.

ClaireBear watched her brothers closely. She was sure that JaJa would not come up with something nice to say about her, but still, she wanted to be ready with her compliments for him and BJ.

When Sunday came, the children were seated early in the family room, waiting for their parents to join them for their first family meeting hour. It was difficult for them to sit still. They felt uneasy as they waited for their parents because they did not know what to expect.

Mr. Bob and Ms. Carol entered the family room and sat in single chairs facing ClaireBear, JaJa, and BJ. Mr. Bob began to speak. "I want to thank everyone for being here on time. Before we start, I want you to know that your mom and I noticed a little less bickering during the week. We are proud of you," said Mr. Bob. "Yes, that's right," said Ms. Carol. "In fact, we are not asking you to do anything that we are unwilling to do ourselves. We also have a list of compliments of behavior that we noticed from all of you during the week."

Mr. Bob and Ms. Carol took turns reading off their list of nice things they noticed about each kid during the week. They also mentioned how they felt when they saw it. Each child had several detailed compliments. Mr. Bob and Ms. Carol spoke with kindness and a spirit of love.

Mr. Bob and Ms. Carol had set the tone for the rest of the meeting. The children felt loved and appreciated when they heard all the nice things their parents said about them. They began to relax and believe that FMH was not so horrible after all.

The children were told to start their compliments with the words, "This week, I noticed." ClaireBear went first. She faced JaJa and said, "This week, I noticed that you took the time to help BJ with his homework. That was cool," JaJa smiled at ClaireBear because it was a nice thing to say, and it was unexpected. Then, ClaireBear faced BJ and said, "This week, I noticed that you put all your toys away neatly without Mommy telling you to do it." After hearing this, BJ smiled at ClaireBear pridefully.

Now, it was BJ's turn. He looked a little upset because
ClaireBear said the same compliment to JaJa that
he was going to say. BJ turned his attention to
ClaireBear. He said, "This week, I noticed that when
I asked you to race me to the pole at the corner,
you said ok. You won the race, but that was fun.
And JaJa, I know that ClaireBear said this already,
but this week I noticed that you are really smart
in math and helped me with my math homework."
After hearing this, JaJa gave BJ a goofy smile.

Then, it was JaJa's turn to give his compliments. He faced BJ and said, "This week, I noticed that you're the first one to say good morning to me every day, even when I'm grouchy sometimes. You're a cool little brother." Everyone smiled when JaJa gave BJ his compliment. In the past, that was something that JaJa took for granted. The time came for JaJa to give ClaireBear her compliment. All week long, she wondered if he had anything good to say to her. JaJa faced ClaireBear with a serious look on his face. ClaireBear's whole body became tense while she waited for him to speak. What he said came as a surprise to everyone. He said, "ClaireBear, this week I noticed that your friend Fatima was very upset. She was crying about something. I didn't hear what you said to her, but I saw you put your arm around her and said something to make her feel better. You're a good friend. Plus, you always look out for me and BJ." Upon hearing this, ClaireBear had a lump in her throat, and her eyes became watery. She didn't want to cry, so she held back her tears in front of JaJa and the rest of the family. With a shaky voice, ClaireBear said, "Thank you, JaJa."

44

In the next few meetings, ClaireBear, JaJa, and BJ came up with a list of two or more sincere compliments for FMH. They wanted to make sure to have extra just in case someone else had the same compliment. During this time, Mr. Bob and Ms. Carol noticed that the children still argued with each other once in a while, but for the most part, they were getting along great.

Four months later, ClaireBear, JaJa, and BJ had made a habit of noticing the good in each other and making it known even when they were not at the family meeting.

During dinner, Mr. Bob and Ms. Carol told the children that they no longer needed FMH every week. The kids were neither glad nor sad about the news. ClaireBear, JaJa, and BJ still noticed the flaws in each other, but they focused more on the whole person and not just the little black dots.

48

Later that night, while everyone else was sleeping, Ms. Carol reflected on their last family meeting hour. Even though it was difficult for the children to embrace FMH initially, Ms. Carol was glad that she and her husband didn't give up. She smiled as she thought of the progress that ClaireBear, JaJa and BJ had made as she drifted off to sleep.

Children's books by Cynthia Dewindt

The Dewavery Way
(Ms. Carol Sings the ABC's)

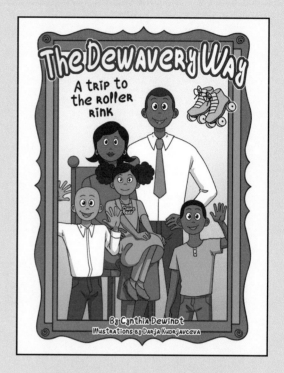

The Dewavery Way
(A Trip to the Roller Rink)

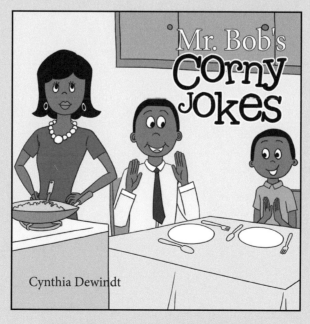

Mr. Bob's Corny Jokes

Printed in the United States
by Baker & Taylor Publisher Services